For Jacqui

First published 2022 by Nosy Crow Ltd
The Crow's Nest, 14 Baden Place, Crosby Row, London SE1 1YW, UK
Nosy Crow Eireann Ltd, 44 Orchard Grove, Kenmare, Co Kerry, V93 FY22, Ireland
www.nosycrow.com

ISBN 978 1 83994 499 4

Nosy Crow and associated logos are trademarks and/or
registered trademarks of Nosy Crow Ltd.

A CIP catalogue record for this book is available from
the British Library.

Printed in China
Papers used by Nosy Crow are made from wood grown
in sustainable forests.

10 9 8 7 6 5 4 3 2 1

WE DISAGREE ABOUT THIS TREE

ROSS COLLINS

nosy crow

How wonderful – you got a tree!

Now just **relax** and you will see
how **Christmassy**
a tree can be
with decoration
left to **me**.

While this is nice to some degree, your baubles seem too **large** to me. Now step aside and **you** will see just how to do this properly.

Your tree is **much too glittery!**
It is so bright
I cannot see!

So let's save electricity,
and leave the decor
up to me.

Your love of tinsel's plain to see,
but it's not how a tree should be.
If we had hired
a referee,
I'm sure that they
would side with me.

Oh goodness me,
this cannot be!

These candles are
incendiary!

It has become

quite clear to me,

we **disagree**

about this tree.

I like a fairy normally,
but not when it's a manatee!
This doesn't fill me
full of glee.
We disagree
about this tree.

Now what is this insanity?
Our tree's defying gravity!
It's creaking quite alarmingly!

Quick!
Over here!
Stand back with me!

What happens
when we disagree?
It all just ends
disastrously!

But what is **this**
that I can see?
Two presents
where our tree should be!

On this, at least,
we **can** agree . . .
these jumpers suit us
perfectly!

We have a **perfect** Christmas tree,
when I'm with **you** and you're with **me**.

Merry Christmas!